Bubbles

By:

Moira Arsenault

To order additional copies of this book, contact:
Xlibris Corporation
1-888-795-4274
www.Xlibris.com
Orders@Xlibris.com

Special Thank You

I would love to give a whole hearted thank you to all who have supported me in this venture. My publisher for enjoying this book and printing it for me. Shelley who got my 'feet' on the path to the right publisher. My family and friends for the confidence, excitement and extra little nudges, Tracey, Tiffany, Crystal, Dean, Barb, Mal, Cindy, Ana, John and Donna. My Father, Frank (RIP) for having me promise him to get it published. My children, Abby, Kyle, Alyssa, Travis and Katelyn for inspiring me, keeping me young and creative. I especially would like to thank my wonderful loving husband for believing in me, encouraging me and for helping me to see my own potential. Dreams do come true!

I see bubbles here and there,

Bubbles, bubbles everywhere.

I see bubbles in the tub,

In I get, glub, glub, glub.

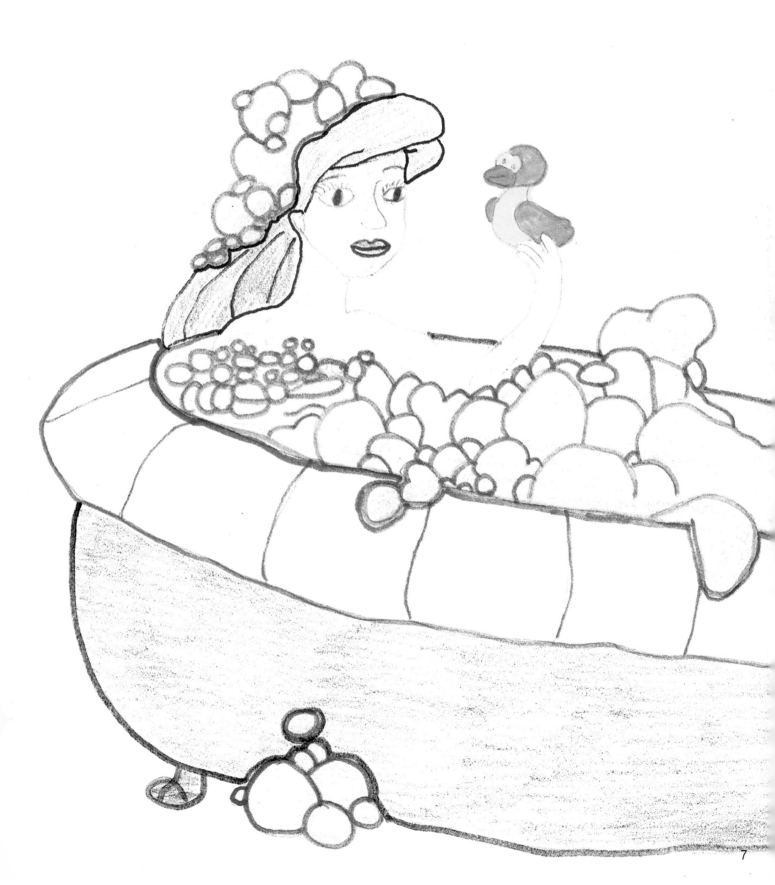

I see bubbles on the car,

Can you see where they are?

I see bubbles in the sink,

Made from soap that was pink.

I see bubbles on my hands,

That wash away mud and sand.

I see bubbles, in the air,

Do not break them, play with care.

I see bubbles on the floor,

In the bucket you'll see more.

I see bubbles in the wash.

Are those my clothes? Oh my gosh!

Bubbles, bubbles here and there.

Do you see bubbles anywhere?

Edwards Brothers,Inc!
Thorofare, NJ 08086
17 February, 2011
BA2011048